Teddy in the
Undersea Kingdom

QUALITY TIME BOOKS™

TEDDY TALES:

Teddy in the Undersea Kingdom
Teddy's Christmas Gift
When Teddy Woke Early
Teddy and the Chinese Dragon

Library of Congress Cataloging-in-Publication Data

Mogensen, Jan.
   Teddy in the undersea kingdom.

   (Teddy tales) (Quality time books)
   Translation of: Eventyr på havets bund.
   Summary: While visiting the undersea kingdom of the royal clam family, Teddy daringly rescues the little clam princess from the wicked King Crab.
   [1. Teddy bears — Fiction. 2. Clams — Fiction. 3. Beaches — Fiction] I. Title. II. Series.
PZ7.M7274Tf   1985   [E]   85-26093
ISBN 1-55532-001-5
ISBN 1-55532-000-7 (lib. bdg.)

North American edition first published in 1985 by

Gareth Stevens Children's Books
RiverCenter Building, Suite 201
1555 North RiverCenter Drive
Milwaukee, Wisconsin 53212, USA

U.S. edition copyright © 1985
Text copyright © 1985 by Gareth Stevens, Inc.
Illustrations copyright © 1984 by Jan Mogensen

First published as *Eventyr pa havets bunds* in Denmark by Borgen with an original text copyright by Jan Mogensen

English text: MaryLee Knowlton

Printed in the United States of America

Teddy in the Undersea Kingdom

Jan Mogensen

Gareth Stevens Publishing
Milwaukee

Teddy sat on the beach. Max and Norah were swimming and splashing in the waves. Teddy thought he would just watch. If the truth be known, he was a little afraid of the water.

"You never know what is on the bottom of the sea," he told himself. "Maybe crabs would bite my toes!"

As the afternoon passed, the bright sun and the sparkling water tired Teddy's eyes. He closed them for just a moment and listened to Max and Norah shouting to each other in the water.

Teddy felt it suddenly become very quiet on the beach. He sat up and looked around. The beach was deserted. The sun was setting and the sea was very still.

"Where are Max and Norah?" he thought, frightened for a minute. Then he told himself bravely, "I won't worry. They always come back for me."

He picked up his red bucket and fishing net and headed toward the water.

Teddy walked along the shoreline looking for treasures. A shapely snail caught his eye and he put it in his bucket for Max.

Near it a pebble sparkled. "Probably gold," Teddy thought. "I will give it to Norah."

Teddy straightened up to stretch his back. Before him appeared a magnificent sand castle with spires and towers and a long bridge leading to the shore.

"Anyone with a place this big must want company," the little bear told himself. "I'm going visiting."

Inside, Teddy waited to be greeted.

"Is anyone here?" he called. "I'm visiting, you know." No one answered.

As the sound of his voice died away, Teddy thought he heard crying deep inside the castle.

Teddy walked through long halls till he came to a large room. At the top of a long staircase sat the King Clam and the Queen Clam. Surrounding them were scores of clam princes and princesses.

Everyone was crying, but they all said welcome the best they could.

"Good afternoon," Teddy said, and bowed. "Why are you all in such a gloomy mood?"

The King Clam looked at Teddy with sad eyes. "Something terrible has happened," he began. "Today, when our littlest princess was running on the beach, the King Crab took her. Now he is holding her captive in his cave at the bottom of the sea."

"I can certainly do something about that!" Teddy told him bravely.

"I will need a swift fish to carry me," he announced. "I am going to bring your princess home."

The royal clam family stopped crying. They led Teddy down to the shore, where a strong, swift fish waited. Teddy climbed on her back.

"To the King Crab's cave!" he shouted. And the fish moved smoothly through the waves and under the sea.

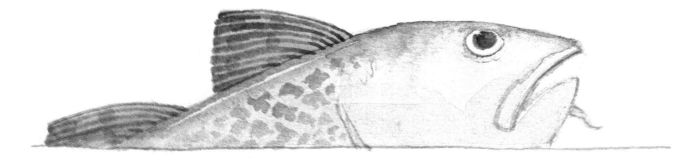

The fish carried Teddy deep into the sea. Finally they came to some strange, tall plants that swayed from side to side like a moving fence.

"What is that?" Teddy asked.

"Seaweed," said the fish. "Through the seaweed, under the green stone, is the King Crab's cave."

The fish stopped at the door to the King Crab's cave.

"You'll have to go in alone," she said. "This is your adventure, not mine. Good luck!"

Teddy moved quietly toward the cave. He laid his fishing net just outside the entrance and covered it with sand.

Stepping back, he yelled, "Give me that clam princess, you sappy sidewalker!"

"Nobody calls me a sappy sidewalker and gets away with all his toes!" screamed the King Crab. And he dashed from his cave!

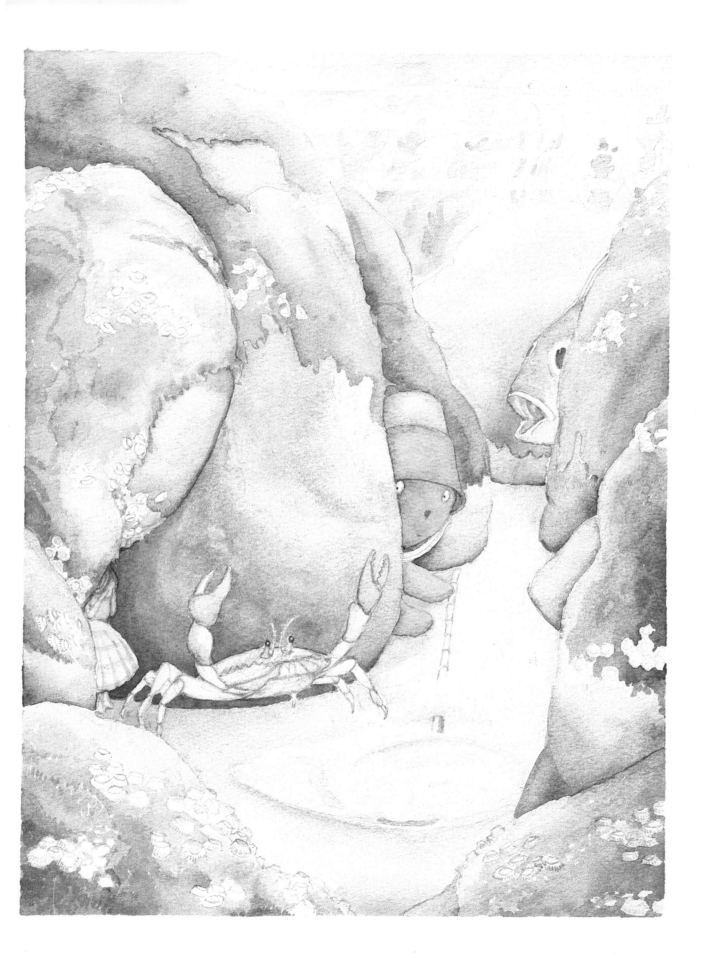

The crab stopped at the cave opening. Teddy lifted the net in a wink and twisted it closed. Then he rescued the little clam princess from the cave.

"I'll let you go if you promise to stay away from the clam family," he told the angry crab.

"My word of honor as a king," came the quiet reply.

"Good!" said Teddy, opening the net, "because I want to take my fishing net home."

"Come, Fish!" he shouted. "Take us to the royal clam castle!"

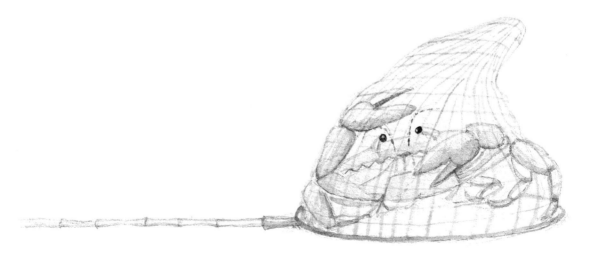

Night had fallen when they arrived at the harbor. The royal clam family let out a cheer.

The Queen Clam hugged the little princess.

"Thank you, Teddy!" she said. "You have made our lives bright again."

"Please take this with our thanks," said the King Clam, removing his fine conch crown.

Teddy blushed. He didn't know what to say, so he bowed.

At that, all the royal clams threw their hats in the air and cheered, "Teddy! Teddy!"

"Teddy! Teddy!"

That voice sounded familiar. Teddy opened his eyes. The castle, the royal clams, and the big fish had all disappeared. Norah knelt before him with a big conch in her hand.

"Look, Teddy! See what we found down by the water. A real conch."

"Hold it to your ear. You can hear it whispering," said Max. "Some people say you can hear adventures from the bottom of the sea."